RIVER SUMMER

MEYARI MCFARLAND

SPECIAL OFFER

The rainbow has infinite shades, just as this collection covers the spectrum of fictional possibilities.

From contemporary romances like *The Shores of Twilight Bay* to dark fantasy like *A Lone Red Tree* and out to SF futures in *Child of Spring*, *Iridescent* covers the gamut of time, space and genre.

Meyari McFarland shows her mastery in this first omnibus collection of her short fiction. Twenty-five amazing stories, all with queer characters going on adventures, solving mysteries, and falling in love are here in the first Rainbow Collection.

And now you can get this massive collection of short queer fiction, all of it with the happy endings you love, *for free!*

Sign up here for your free copy of Iridescent now!

CONTENTS

Other Books by Meyari McFarland:	vii
River Summer	1
Author's Note: Fighting the Morrigan's Hand	17
1. Coming Ashore	18
2. Conflicting Mandates	27
Other Books by Meyari McFarland:	35
Afterword	37
Author Bio	39

OTHER BOOKS BY MEYARI MCFARLAND:

Day Hunt on the Final Oblivion

Day of Joy

Immortal Sky

A New Path

Following the Trail

Crafting Home

Finding a Way

Go Between

Like Arrows of Fate

Out of Disaster

The Shores of Twilight Bay

Coming Together

Following the Beacon

The Solace of Her Clan

You can find these and many other books at www.MDR-Publishing.com. We are a small independent publisher focusing on LGBT content. Please sign up for our mailing list to get regular updates on the latest preorders and new releases and a free ebook!

Copyright ©2024 by Mary Raichle

Print ISBN: 978-1-64309-103-7

Cover image

Illustration 194639185 © Lvqi Peng | Dreamstime.com

All rights reserved. No part of this publication may be reproduced or transmitted in any form or by any means, electronic or mechanical, including photocopy, recording or any information storage and retrieval system, without permission in writing from the publisher.

Requests for permission to make copies of any part of the work should be emailed to publisher@mdr-publishing.com.

This book is also available in TPB format from all major retailers.

❦ Created with Vellum

This story is dedicated to my husband, always.

RIVER SUMMER

Water lapped against the side of the barge, slapping, gurgling, endlessly burbling along against the hull. It sang of the fish along the riverbed, the snake-heads lazily flowing up and down the River. Mer song echoed through its yammering, clicking, shouting, singing, laughing in exact counterpoint to the water's ever-present song.

Duru wrapped his pillow around his head. He just wanted some sleep. Was that too much to ask? The muddy water didn't have to grab his magic and force him to listen. It never used to back when he lived on land. Why couldn't it stop already, just for a few hours so that he could sleep?

It never stopped. The sound continued whether the barge was moving or docked, heavy load or none at all. Weird that a sound that didn't exist could be so overwhelming that you flat couldn't ignore it, no matter what you did.

Eirian always had claimed that it was soothing, that never-ending murmur of noise. He'd dance on the deck, laughing and spinning so that the rainbow of ribbons decorating his vest flung out like the shock of reddish-brown dreads that came down to his waist whenever he let them loose.

River-song was the music of his soul.

Color and life and movement, warm and bright and happy, that was Eirian. He was as brown as his River, as full of life as its murky depths. To him, there was no joy without River-song lifting him up and buoying him along.

But Eirian and been born on the River. Born there, grew up daring the parasites and snake-heads that could swallow a grown man whole. He'd sworn he felt odd every time he left the river, walked the shore, stood in a building that didn't shift under his feet.

Duru couldn't imagine that.

No.

He could. He was living it, in the opposite. What Duru wouldn't give to have solid ground right about how. Where Eirian was life and movement, Duru had always been as solid as a granite boulder, as dark as obsidian and as quiet as the night after a festival where everyone had drunk, smoked and fucked themselves to sleep.

Water smacked against the barge hull right next to Duru's ear, shouting that he needed to pay attention.

He groaned and pushed the pillow off, shoved the thin blanket off and swung his feet out of his bunk. Their bunk. Still a new thought, sharing a bunk, especially when Duru had so much exhaustion crusting his eyes.

Duru held a breath before letting the wonder and fear of a shared bunk go slow and easy, just the way Ama had taught him when she took him to pray. Hold a thought in your heart, breathe in, out, consign that thought to the Higher Powers.

Didn't work to fix anything because Higher Powers didn't see any profit in fixing things for people what had no money or power. Duru Palmer and his entire family always had been and always would be nobodies existing at the margins of the systems that held the world together. They might be gifted, but only in things that didn't matter.

He didn't count. He wasn't real. No Higher Power would give a good goddamn if Duru prayed for real.

Well.

Duru was nobody for real now. He laughed and scrubbed his hands over his face, feeling the new scars that had stopped pulling every time he made a face. They caught under his fingers, dragged against his palms.

If he chanced a look in the tiny scrap of polished silver Eirian used as a mirror, those scars would stand out like inked in gouges in his face. They were ugly on his stomach, if more welcome given that they'd taken unwanted organs after the explosion that "killed" him. Had to be worse on his face. Duru didn't look. He was just grateful that the scars were bad enough no one would recognize him right off if they looked at him.

There was no one back on shore who'd look for Duru. Why look for the dead?

If Eirian hadn't been river born and bred, Duru would've died. Eirian's prayers held power. Eirian's pleas had brought healing energy at the cost of Duru's unwanted womb. More than a fair trade, though Duru still wished it hadn't come at the cost of his family's death, too.

Duru shook his head against that spiraling whirlpool of thought, got up with his head down so that he wouldn't crack his skull on the dark, heavy beams overhead, and pulled on his pants. Binder was a wiggle and struggle to lace it down flat enough for the spells to engage, but no way was Duru going out without it. A loose vest over-top made him outright overdressed for the river but more comfortable in his skin. It disguised the scars on his stomach and back.

The binder hid itself once the spells engaged.

"Thought you were sleeping," Eirian said from his spot up at the wheel.

"Couldn't," Duru said without meeting the worry that had taken root in Eirian's eyes.

He looked out over the River instead.

Looked like a lake to Duru. It was wide enough here that each shore was a bare line along the horizon. The brown, muddy water slipped under their barge, slapping against the hull like it was daring Duru to take a dip. Or to dive to his actual death instead of the presumed death everyone on-shore thought he'd gone to.

A rippling dark rainbow fin as long as Duru was tall cut through the roiling surface of the water.

Not close. A good hundred yards off which meant that the snake-head was easily ten times the length of the barge. Duru pressed his lips together, turning to Eirian who nodded towards the head of the barge.

"Can you check the mer?" Eirian asked with apologetic grimness twisting his genial smile into a grimace. "They like you."

"They like scaring me," Duru said, nodding that of course he would.

"That, too," Eirian agreed.

This grin was one hundred percent a real one. Duru rolled his eyes, noting that Eirian's hands on the wheel were calm, loose, not white-knuckled at all. Okay then. Snake-head but maybe not a threat to worry about.

The barge had nothing on deck today. Tomorrow they'd pull into Tamboli, pick up a load, drop off the crates waiting below-decks in the cold and dark of the hold. For now, the deck was fifty feet of polished wood impregnated with tar and resin. Duru's feet missed the many cleats for tying down crates automatically. His eyes were all on the water in front of the barge where the mer swam and pulled at the barge.

No one jumping. That was good. Jumping meant predators under the surface. A good number of colorful fins slicing up through the surface of the water but all of those were young ones, the juveniles who were learning barge work while their elders pulled. The team of ten that were in the harnesses right now rippled the surface with the thrusts of their huge tails but didn't break it.

He'd asked about that the first time Eirian sent him up to check on the mer. Why be so careful about the surface? Air didn't hurt mer. They could beach themselves, sun, spend hours, even days out of the water if they wanted.

The eldest mer, matriarch of the pod, had clicked laughs that set the entire pod off into belly laughs that rippled the water for yards and yards and yards around the barge. Tendai had grinned with needle-sharp teeth at Duru, great saucer eyes making half-moon shapes as her grin stretched her mouth three quarters the way around her sleek pointed head.

Nothing intelligent should look that different. Mer smiles still made Duru want to run screaming back onto solid ground, never mind that it'd be as sure death as jumping into a snake-head's mouth.

"Wasted effort," Tendai had replied finally. "No one but a minnow would waste energy by trying to swim through air. No bite to the tail in the air. Just noise and splash to pull in hungry snake-heads."

Duru knelt down at the front of the barge, rapping on the hull until one of the juveniles surfaced and grinned that gape-mouth, needle-tooth, too-wide grin at him.

"Eirian wanted to know if the snake-head is a problem," Duru said.

The juvenile slipped under the surface and then jumped right out of the water, giving Duru a glimpse of the cream-yellow belly and streaked green-brown flanks that marked

Kita, the oldest juvenile. The little ones were all were dappled, like spots of sunlight dancing on an old bed of leaves. When a mer grew up, they lost the dapples, developed stripes and their fins grew longer.

So did the claws on their sinuous arms.

Duru jerked and cursed as Kita leaped up out of the water and right onto the nose of the barge. Her tail dragged in the water, pulling the barge down on that side enough to make Duru dig his feet in so he didn't slide straight into Kita's too-wide needle-toothed mouth. She was half the length of the barge, all sinuous muscle, claws and teeth, with toxic slime that would drive Duru mad if he let it rest on his skin for too long.

She stretched her neck and nodded to Duru. It put her face way too close to Duru's for his comfort, especially when she dragged a slate-grey tongue over her left eyeball and then grinned at him again.

"Not bad," Kita said. She held onto the deck with those foot-long claws, digging them into the wood so that she wouldn't be dragged right back into the water by the River's grip on her tail. "Didn't scream this time."

"Kita," Duru groaned.

She click-laughed at him, no apology in sight. "Snake-head is Old Man Snake. Been following barge all this time. No biting, no poking, no sign is hungry. Belly is still swollen from last meal. Should be okay. Tendai thinks is pacing barge and heading up to spawning grounds."

"…Oh." Duru tried to find something else to say to that.
Failed.

Kita laughed, her clicks sending the other juveniles into jumping and splashing and laughing along with her. She licked her other eye and then let go of the deck, sliding back down into the water so smoothly that there was barely a ripple. Duru sat there, heart pounding, until the slime of

Kita's belly started to dry and flake away in the filtered morning sun.

Then he got up and headed back to Eirian who's hands were white-knuckle on the wheel again. Duru deliberately went behind Eirian, wrapped his arms around Eirian's lean waist and then whined. Pressed his forehead against Eirian's back while doing it.

Eirian laughed at Duru, just like Kita and the juvenile mer had.

But his shoulders relaxed, and his hands weren't white-knuckle when Duru lifted his head and put his chin on Eirian's shoulder. Good enough. Last thing Duru wanted was Eirian getting lost in the waking nightmares he'd been prone to since everything went bad for Duru.

"What'd Kita say?" Eirian asked.

"She called the snake-head Old Man Snake," Duru said.

Eirian dropped the wheel, letting it spin as it would for a terrifying second as he turned to stare at Duru with his jaw dropped open. Then he snapped back around, grabbed the wheel and straightened it out so that the mer wouldn't think he suddenly wanted to change direction.

"Old Man Snake? You're sure?" Eirian asked in a harder voice than Duru had heard from him in months. It was like being in the middle of the wars again and made Duru's stomach churn just like back then, too.

"That's what she said," Duru said. He shrugged. "It's Old Man Snake, belly full and no signs of hunger. No poking or biting. She said that exactly, I think. Apparently, Tendai thinks he's heading upriver to the spawning grounds."

"Old Man Snake isn't gonna spawn," Eirian said in that hard, hard voice. "Old Man Snake isn't flesh and blood like we are. Or like the mer are. Old Man Snake is a Higher Power, Duru. How long has he been pacing us?"

"Um..." Duru hesitated and then winced when Eirian's

eyes went wide. "All along? Kita said, what was it? Oh, yeah. She said he'd "been following barge all along". So... maybe since the last town?"

"No," Eirian whispered, eyes staring over the barge deck towards the ripples where Tendai and her pod pulled the barge. "All along is longer than that. Since... I don't know. Take the wheel. I have to ask Tendai myself."

Duru's heart half-stopped. "I can't pilot! I don't have the gift for it!"

"It's not piloting," Eirian snapped. "Hold this handle and this handle. Keep your elbows at your waist. Don't shift around more than you have to. Just hold straight. I trust you more than I trust leashing the wheel for something like this. If I go into the water, hit the stick and stop the barge."

Duru's heart all-stopped, leaving him gasping through an echoing grey tunnel until Eirian's hands on his shoulder shook him back from a faint.

"Don't go in the water," Duru begged.

"Duru, I won't unless I have to," Eirian promised. His hands cupped Duru's scarred face as if he'd never nearly gotten his head blown off. "It'll be okay."

"No," Duru whispered, clinging to Eirian's hands which really should be on the wheel. "No, you don't understand. Don't go in the water. Don't. Don't do that. Please, don't do that."

Everything came with a price.

Everything. Eirian who'd lived his whole life on the River didn't believe it. Didn't feel it in his blood and bones. The River took things away, swept them out to the sea, and brought other things to replace it. Easy come, easy go, that was life on the River.

But it wasn't real. It wasn't true. Everything came at a price. Sometimes the price was cheap, easy, but most of the time it was too high. More than anyone would want to pay.

Duru clung to Eirian's hands, trying to figure out words that would explain.

"The River-song has been so loud," Duru said as he stared into Eirian's eyes. "Loud and demanding. It wants something. Not Old Man Snake. Not the mer. Not the fish or the monsters or even the ground underneath. The River, Eirian. It *wants*. Its waiting. Don't go in the water. That's an offering. That's giving it something. It'll take. We... We've given so much already. Please!"

Eirian's eyes went wider and wider until he looked like he had mer blood, impossible as that was. He turned and looked at the River and only then did Duru realize that Eirian had hooked one ankle around the wheel so that it wouldn't spin.

He let go of Duru's face. Stood on two legs and held the wheel with one strong, lean hand burned oak-brown by the sun. Stared at the water.

Then hit the stick, the one that unhooked the mer's harnesses so that the barge would stop.

Tendai surfaced, ears flaring like wings as she surged forward without the weight of the barge. She flipped and came back to catch the barge so that it wouldn't start spinning round sideways in the current. The other mer worked with her, Kita directing the juveniles to put down the anchors that usually hung on the sides of the barge until they stopped for the night or came to a town.

"Problem?" Tendai asked, drifting back so that her massive head rested just at the stairwell leading down into the hold. That put her tail flaring and shifting in the water well to the stern of the barge, half again the length the barge behind the rudder.

"Duru's been hearing the River-song," Eirian said in a far-distant voice that had just a hint of song to it. "It's... not happy."

"River-song?" Tendai asked, this time looking right at

Duru who winced and squirmed while rubbing his belly where the River and Eirian's magic had taken away his womb while saving his life. "How long?"

"Since ever," Duru said with a little shrug. "I always hear water. And wind, and earth. Fire's too fast. I don't hear it as much as feel it pushing at me. It's always there. But it's different now…"

Tendai nodded slowly. One long sinuous arm came out of the water. She pointed at Duru's belly with the two-foot claw that tipped her finger.

"Yeah," Duru admitted. "Since then. Since I gave up having babies. Since I sacrificed all the babies I could ever have. You know, to live."

Tendai sunk down in the water until just her saucer eyes were above the surface of the muddy water.

Out further in the heart of the current, Old Man Snake surfaced. His long tail-body lazily undulated in the water, holding him even with the barge. Where Tendai and Kita had faces almost like a human's, close enough to make Duru's stomach go to knots, Old Man Snake had a face like a croc, long snout bisected by gashed-open mouth filled with knife-shaped teeth. His mane sprouted in a cloud of wiggling not-hairs around his chin and ears. The horns on his head branched once, twice, on to six points. More than any snake-head had.

Very old Old Man River.

Duru stared at him, heart pounding.

Old Man River tilted his head to the side as if considering Duru. Or maybe considering what Duru wasn't saying, what Duru feared, all the quiet and loud and endless terrors of the Higher Powers that had shaped his family and then taken their lives when the war came though.

"You are owed," Old Man River murmured.

Duru gasped and dropped to his knees. The sound came

from the water. The air. The creatures living within the River including Tendai and Kita and the rest of the mer. It was music and life and spawning and death, all wrapped up in the ever-shifting flow of the water underneath, around, beside the barge.

"No," Duru whispered. He felt Eirian's arms around him but couldn't see him. Couldn't feel. There was only the River, Old Man River, talking straight to his mind.

"Yes," Old Man River replied. "You are owed. Many lives given, only one life returned."

Duru gasped for breath around a sob that tore through his scarred gut, up his lungs and out into the air. Drowning, he was drowning. The weight of the River was pushing him down into the muck below. He'd never see the sun again, never burn his skin working the barge with Eirian, never curl up with him in their bunk as the barge gently rocked them to sleep.

"Duru!"

Eirian's voice was so far away. He grabbed for Eirian's hand, swallowing metal as he sucked air into lungs convinced they were filled with murky brown water.

Duru dragged another breath in. Pushed the River out. Breathed in, River out.

It worked, slowly, painfully, just as it was supposed to. Human souls weren't strong enough to talk direct to Higher Powers and Old Man River felt older and stronger than any Duru had touched before. Even bringing down lightning from the Sky Goddess' bower during the war hadn't been this hard. That was fast.

This was slow. Inevitable. Sucking him down as he flailed his way back towards the surface of the River's magic.

"Duru, Duru, come back, come back," Eirian whispered in Duru's ear. "Don't drown. Don't give in."

"Owed." Duru gasped, coughed blood, and then gasped again. "Owed. Gave many lives and only got one."

"Well… you did," Eirian said. His brown eyes were dark with tears cutting salty tracks down his cheeks. "That's… what happened."

"No," Duru said. He laughed and coughed more blood. "No. I never wanted kids. Never. Those weren't real lives. They'd never have souls. There wasn't ever gonna be a baby from me. I just… I'm glad it's gone. I'm glad it's all gone."

Old Man River hummed, the water rippling along the hull of the drum like the riff starting a dance in the temple during the full moon. "Owed."

"No," Duru said, eyes firmly shut so that he wouldn't meet Old Man River's eyes again and be lost to the current for good this time. "I'm not. My family was owed. They're dead. My whole town, our clan, everyone is dead. There's no one to take the payment, no one to repay the debt to. I just…"

"What?" Tendai asked. Her voice was all underwater, all mournful wail and frightened moan.

"I want the war not to have happened," Duru said. "I want the Holy City to still stand. I want the killing to have been stopped before it turned into slaughter. I want the temples to stand, the stilt-houses to still be there. I want the prayers to still be sung. I want it not to have happened."

He sighed and curled in Eirian's arms. He'd never said it out loud. Not when he was bleeding out. Not when Eirian used the sacrifice of his organs to save his life. Not since. Not once.

What point was there to it?

"You will change it all?" Old Man River asked.

"I can't," Duru protested. "I couldn't then. I can't now. I didn't have the power. I could choose to leave the temples and join Eirian on the River, yes, but that won't stop the war.

I don't have the power to change it, then or now or in the future."

He kept his eyes shut but that didn't stop him from knowing that Old Man River reared up so that his massive lethal head loomed over the barge. Tendai and the mer all darted under the water, swimming away as fast as they could. They should. No Higher Power, especially one as powerful as Old Man River, wanted to be held by a human for longer than it took to complete a boon.

"Who could?" Eirian asked.

The River seemed to go still and solid as if it had frozen from rippled surface right down to the rock under the much below. Duru pulled back and stared into Eirian's eyes. They danced like rain droplets hitting a still pond, moving and rippling through oil-sheen rainbows as his power came alive.

"Who… could?" Duru asked, blinking and blinking and blinking. "I…"

Who could?

That. That was a good question, a better question than anything Duru had come up with. He pulled out of Eirian's arms. Sat with his legs splayed out and his arms supporting him as he leaned back and stared into Old Man River's waiting eyes.

They danced with the same oil-sheen rainbows, but Old Man River's croc smile stretched into true joy as Duru blinked.

"Not my family," Duru said. "They're trapped by our magic, our gifts."

He scrambled to his feet. Ran down the stairs to the main deck. Everywhere his feet touched, lines of stary light bloomed. Duru breathed in the moist, heavy air that wasn't really air. Up by the wheel, Eirian laughed as he began to drum against his thighs. Eirian leaped to his feet and began to dance, heels drumming out the old songs of power and sight and choice. Festival of mid-winter when the River nearly froze, a film of ice creeping out from the stilts and the eels ran under your dugout.

Duru nodded and began to spin in the Mid-Winter dance. He couldn't choose. He didn't know who it should be. Someone strong. Someone desperate. Someone with too much taken and nothing to lose. An ally? Maybe. Soul bound warriors who lost everything when the Holy City fell.

Old Man River hummed as the water drummed against the sides of the barge.

"I give it away," Duru sang as he hit the heart of the Mid-Winter dance. "I give it all away. Save them all, Old Man River. Find the ones who will save it all and give it to them!"

Sound exploded through Duru.

Water lapped against the side of the barge, slapping, gurgling, endlessly burbling along against the hull.

Duru raised his head. The thin blanket tangled around his legs fought as he rolled over and then out of his and Eirian's bunk. He cracked his head against the dark, heavy beam overhead. Clutching his head, Duru collapsed back onto the bunk, breath hissing between his teeth. Filtered sunlight from high clouds overhead shafted down the stairwell.

Just as it had when he couldn't sleep.

"What… did it…?" Duru bit his lip, wincing as his teeth locked onto a spot already bitten through.

Binder, pants, vest overtop; Duru ran up the stairs and found the barge unchanged. The River in front of them rippled from Tendai and the mer pulling them forward. No crates on the deck but he could see the outline of Tamboli at the curve of the River.

"Weren't you sleeping?" Eirian asked as Duru ran up the stairs and looked across the River for Old Man River.

Nothing. No sign of the impossibly long fin. The water

didn't demand, didn't expect, didn't slap against the hull to get Duru's attention.

"I dreamed," Duru said, staring over the River.

"Of what?" Eirian asked.

His eyes were warm and curious, his smile genial and delighted in everything that Duru was. When he took one hand from the wheel, Eirian trailed fingers across Duru's cheek.

Not one scar caught under his fingertips.

Duru rubbed his belly. Those scars were still there. It was…

…The world shifted as his soul caught up to the changes. Or maybe the changes caught up to his soul. Duru shook his head, kissing Eirian's palm.

"It doesn't matter," Duru said. "It's fading anyway. How far up the River will we go this time?"

"Mmm, we can go back to the Holy City if you want," Eirian said thoughtfully. "I should be able to get a load headed up that way."

Duru stared at him for a long enough moment that Eirian frowned and cocked his head like a parrot about to bite. "No. No, let's go back south. I can visit my family later. In a year or two."

"Ha!" Eirian laughed. "Fine by me. Your mother looked like she wanted to gut me for stealing you away from your temple. Let's go all the way to the sea this time. Tendai and the mer will like that. All new fish to hunt out there."

"That sounds perfect," Duru said.

He moved behind Eirian and wrapped his arms around Eirian's waist. It was a coward's path, maybe, but Duru would not risk distracting Old Man River and the other Higher Powers from saving the Holy City. Let his family sign to them. Duru would slip away down the River and let the Chosen Heroes work without interference.

Around them, the River sang its endless song. Duru smiled into Eirian's shoulder. Boons didn't always work. It was up to the recipients to use them well. If the Chosen Heroes didn't choose properly, well.

Duru was willing to try again, though he didn't know what he would sacrifice next time.

He'd find something.

If he had to.

AUTHOR'S NOTE: FIGHTING THE MORRIGAN'S HAND

Choosing your own destiny isn't an easy thing. Making that huge choice of where you're going to go and what you're going to do with your life (whether you're a teenager in our world, someone middle-aged and burned out, or someone in a story), is hard.

The thing is that choosing your path isn't something you do once. It's something that happens moment by moment, day by day as you deal with the world around you. Duru got a second chance to make those choices and did better.

Aravel in Fighting the Morrigan's Hand took the chances he was given and wrung them for everything he could get. Then set to work seeing what he could build out of it. He's a fierce, cheerful, stunningly smart young man who invested everything into seeming like a brainless idiot so writing his book was a blast. Especially as I got to watch him solving problems by coming at them sideways, pretty much every single time.

Hope you enjoy the sample!

1. COMING ASHORE

Aravel stood at the bow of the *Harmonious Song*, clinging to the railing. Two tug boats, six women in each, rowed hard as they pulled the *Song* into its berth. They ignored him. So did the *Song's* sailors. Even Captain Bryna paid him no mind. She was too busy shouting orders to reef the sails and get the *Song* ready to tie up.

Which was fine by Aravel. The twin cities of Yuzuki and Masumi on either side of the Strait of Rio were far more interesting than the work the women around him did to secure the *Harmonious Song*. Yuzuki City in Amadi was on the flat side of the Strait. Its buildings were low and broad, built on stilts that put the houses ten to twenty feet above the muddy ground with heavy roofs that reminded him of Idoya. Not surprising, really. They got much the same weather as Idoya, rain, more rain and still more rain with a brief dry season in the depths of winter where they got biting cold.

Masumi City on the right was on the steep hills of Chinwendu. The flat land of Yuzuki's flood plain gave way to hills and then cliffs and then mountains behind that. The rain that put Yuzuki's streets under water half the time came from

Masumi City's hills wringing the clouds dry before they wended their way into dry central Chinwendu where spider silk was harvested and woven into beautiful cloth.

Where Yuzuki City was built on stilts, Masumi City's building foundations were dug deep into the hillsides with deep gullies for gutters and more stairs than streets. Aravel closed his eyes and breathed deep. The smell of salt and sewage had faded the further up the Strait they went. Now the air smelled of rain and fragrant wood fires.

"Ravi!"

Aunt Colleen's shout startled Aravel. He turned and then sighed at Aunt Colleen's glower. Really, you'd think he was a baby the way she fussed over him. Every single port so far Aunt Collen had all but held his hand to keep him from exploring or talking to people. Aravel was fifteen and more than mature enough to handle handsy sailors, rude foreigners and the occasional fist-fight when someone didn't respect his no's. Either the laughing or the arch ones. The women who didn't take a no got a fist to the face and that always ended the problem.

"Yes, Aunt Colleen?" Ravi called back only to finch as her glare went five times as intense.

He sighed and trotted over, causally avoiding sailors, lines and the billowing sails as they were pulled up and reefed. Really, from the way she frowned you would have thought that it was his first time at sea. She caught his elbow and gave him a little shake.

"I thought I told you to stay in your cabin," Aunt Colleen snapped at him.

"And I thought you understood which of us has higher rank in the family and on this ship," Aravel snapped right back at her. "Aunt Colleen, no matter how good you are at the paperwork, and yes, you're amazing, I still outrank you. Mother said so. So did Uncle Jarmon. There's a reason I'm on this mission and you are not going to keep me from fulfilling it."

Her jaw clenched as her eyes went far too angry that he dared to reprimand her publicly. But really, she brought that on herself. She could have insisted on a private conversation. Oh no, let's scold the boy for daring to know his place.

"Mission," Aunt Colleen said so flatly that she called him a liar by implication. "You."

"Of course," Aravel said, smiling the 'you're Delbhana and I loathe you' smile that had gotten him in trouble a few dozen times before back home. And which might still get him slapped if he wasn't careful. "I'm to visit our relatives here and make sure that we still have allies here. Great-Uncle Jarmon has… worries… about things back home. And given the way Chinwendu politics work, it has to be me, not you. Rank, you know. You're not line direct. I'm the only one who is on the *Harmonious Song*."

The anger transmuted into surprise and then worry. Aunt Colleen bit her lip and glanced over at Captain Bryna who had gone pale. Aravel watched them and then sighed. Lovely. Mother or Father or maybe Gavin had been meddlers and decided that he needed to be 'protected'. If it was Father then they'd been ordered to 'shelter' him from anything dangerous on the trip. Gavin would have just outright told them to keep Aravel from fathering any children along the way.

"Who?" Aravel asked. They both looked away and then blushed when he put his hands on his hips. "Who? Come now. You've gotten orders. Who from and what are the orders? I can't do my job if you're working against me."

"Laoise told me to keep you safe," Aunt Colleen said so grudgingly that Aravel wondered if she'd started the journey with bruises from a fist fight between the two of them.

"Your brother Gavin instructed me to ensure that the crew treated you with all respect," Captain Bryna said a moment later, her ears bright red from the force of her blush. Given that he'd spent most of the trip 'entertaining' her instead of the crew Aravel supposed that she'd fulfilled that instruction quite well despite not following the intent of it.

"Well, you're fine," Aravel said to Captain Bryna with an airy little wave of his hand that made her snort a laugh. "I approve of your methodology there. You," he wagged a finger at Aunt Colleen, "are leaving things out. There are ways to keep a man safe that don't involve treating him like a toddler. Besides, you know I can hit as hard as you can."

That got him a grin from Captain Bryna while Aunt Colleen glowered at him. Ah. So she had left things out. Not that it really mattered, not with the gangplank going down and a group of Chinwenduese officials waiting at the end of the dock for them. Aravel bounced on his toes, kilts swishing around his ankles.

"We'll talk about this later," Aravel told Aunt Colleen. "Let's go say hello and do remember, this is primarily a family visit, not a business trip."

"We always do business in port," Aunt Colleen said, glaring at him.

"Of course we do," Aravel said and if he used his breeziest, most air-headed tone of voice, well, she'd brought that on himself with her attitude this trip. Months of this nonsense were long enough. "But that's not the point. That's just what Dana do along with breathing and getting into fights."

Finally, he got a bellowed laugh out of Aunt Collen. Plus a huge grin from Captain Bryna that promptly relaxed the sailors quite a bit. Good. The two of them really did need to calm down. This wasn't that big of a deal. Aravel had been here a half dozen times before. He knew how to talk to his relatives and to the officials in Chinwendu.

He made sure that Aunt Colleen took the lead down the gangplank. She was older and female so that was appropriate. Captain Bryna stayed on board as was proper here. As soon as they were within three yards of the officials, Aunt Colleen stopped and let Aravel go first.

Dock Mistress with two attendants, one male and one non-gendered, both with clipboards and pens at the ready. They all wore the red and black of Great-Grandfather's clan so that made things easier. Aravel could address them as relatives rather than as strangers. The only fillip in the whole thing was the relative age differences between Aravel and the Dock Mistress.

She frowned at Aravel, trying to read his rank in his Dana blue plaid kilt, lack of petticoats and light shirt under a simple Dana blue vest. Every single thing he wore shouted a lack of respect for his family's power but he was on the other side of the world so he didn't have to hobble himself with petticoats and yards of lace if he didn't want to.

Aravel grinned and carefully pulled out the little insignia Great-Uncle Jarmon had given him, attaching it to his vest pocket. It was shaped like a pentagram divided in half. One half, the top, held the Dana triple-swirl done in lapis lazuli and gold. The bottom half held the Tamura family seal, a trio of hand scythes arranged in a bouquet effect, tied with rice straw where the handles crossed. That was done in onyx and silver, making the little insignia a beautiful but very pricy object.

The Dock Mistress let out a tiny sigh of relief, nodding once nearly imperceptibly to Aravel. He nodded back, trying not to smile too broadly. Knowing what rank you held relative to another person was so desperately important in Chinwendu. They bowed at once, Aravel going slightly higher than the Dock Mistress who held the bow half a second longer than he did. Her attendants bowed far more deeply and held it until the Dock Mistress signaled them to stand up with a flick of her fingertips. Hopefully Aunt Colleen could manage herself. Aravel had to trust that she could. She'd taken up a post too far behind him for him to see if she was bowing properly.

"I wish you greetings, cousin of the Dana Family line of Aingeal of Aingeal City," the Dock Mistress said. "I am Damura Kamiko, Dock Mistress of the Trade Docks of Masumi City of Chinwendu, fourth daughter of the third son of the lady of the Damura."

"I thank you for your greetings, elder cousin Tamura Kamiko," Aravel replied. "I am Dana Aravel of the line direct of the Dana Family of Aingeal of Aingeal City, second son of the first daughter of the first daughter of the Dana Clan. This is Dana Colleen, my Grandmother's fourth daughter's second daughter who will be handling the trade and paperwork for Minoo while we are here. I would visit with our relatives at the bequest of my Great-Uncle Jarmon who was first son of Tamura Tau, who married my Great-Grandmother Anwyn and founded our Clan with her in Aingeal."

Kamiko's eyes went wide. She licked her lips and bowed very slightly, conveying her worry quite well without saying a word. Aravel pressed his lips together and let his eyes smile just as much as they wanted to while bowing back just a bit deeper to say that yes, of course she could ask.

"One would hope that the visit is not formal," Kamiko said.

"One would be quite right to worry about that," Aravel replied so brightly that Aunt Colleen snorted behind him and the two attendants shut their eyes and pressed their lips together so that they wouldn't visibly show amusement beyond what was appropriate to their rank. "If the visitor were of greater age. A visit of one below the age of maturity is, of course, never a matter of great formality. And this one," he gestured towards himself with a bright grin that made Kamiko swallow a laugh, "is not yet of age in either Chinwendu or Aingeal. Thus all formalness is avoided and pleasantness can abound for all."

That did get a laugh, not just from Kamiko but from a passing sailor who'd naturally eavesdropped on the conversation while carefully not meeting anyone's eyes. And from the Harbor Mistress, a stern eighty-some year old woman who was broad of shoulder, narrow of hip and flat of bust as most Chinwenduese chosen-women were. She shook her head, coming over to stare at first Aravel's insignia and then at his face for a long moment.

"It has been long since the Dana have sent a formal representative to the port," the Harbor Mistress said to Kamiko but she was really talking to Aravel.

Introductions would be required if they were to speak directly and since she was wearing green and brown, that would mean going through the whole rigmarole of determining exactly where the Dana ranked in Chinwenduese politics today. Versus yesterday or tomorrow or last year. Not worth the bother for anyone, honestly.

Kamiko hummed and nodded, staring thoughtfully into the distance while rocking on her heels. "One forgets how old the eldest son of Damura Tao is now."

"One could be very well excused for that," Aravel said as if talking to the air while Aunt Colleen smothered a laugh in her fist. "Because Dana Jarmon, eldest son, has never admitted to being older than fifty-five even though he has seen seventy-nine summers."

That made both Kamiko and the Harbor Mistress splutter laughs as they pretended not to hear him. Kamiko nodded sagely, eyes sparkling with laughter before she managed to regain a properly formal expression.

"Age does tend to make long travel uncomfortable," Kamiko said as if offering a bit of wisdom from the ages.

"Quite so, quite so," the Harbor Mistress agreed.

She rubbed her back and then chuckled before bowing slightly towards Kamiko and then strolling on up the dock as if she'd merely stopped on her way to her destination. Nicely done, that. It allowed her to both find out what was going on and to leave quickly and efficiently instead of dealing with all the introductions, greetings and goodbyes required between non-family members.

Kamiko snorted, eyes a little hard as she stared at the Harbor Mistress' back. Hmm, perhaps more than just nosiness, then. "Will an escort be needed, eudi-Dana Aravel-duai?"

"Yes, I believe that would be appropriate, aeji-Tamura Kimiko-chu," Aravel replied. He shrugged at her frown. "Orders were given that I was to be kept 'safe'. As euji-Dana Colleen-chu has work here and the Captain and sailors have no link to any Chinwendu families, well, an escort would be necessary. Perhaps one of your attendants can run back and send a message? There is little need to rush. We should be in port for, oh, a time, I believe."

Kamiko looked over Aravel's shoulder to Aunt Colleen who gave him a hard look.

"We should be here for at least two weeks, twenty days, euji-Tamura Kimiko-chai," Aunt Collen said, giving Kimiko the higher rank, unlike Aravel. He could get away with that because of his place in the bloodline. Her lower place in their genealogy meant she had to be properly polite and designate Kimiko as a younger woman with higher rank.

"Ah, my thanks, aeji-Dana Colleen-chu," Kimiko replied. "Our report will state as much. Eudi-Dana Aravel-duai, do please inform me or my staff if your visit will extend longer than that. It will influence the visas for your ship and crew."

"I will, aeji-Tamura Kimiko-chu, I promise," Aravel said with a flirty little bow that made her snort and her attendants grin. The neuter one raised a hand to keep from laughing out loud.

After that, it was a simple thing to get their visas for Captain Bryna and the crew. They were, after all, just slips of paper with the name of the individual, their rank on the ship and the duration of the ship's stay in port, meant to be kept in a pocket until needed for reference. So much easier than visiting Minoo with all their oppressive paperwork.

Of course, Aunt Colleen had to get the numbers of each visa, the names of Kimiko and her staff, and the exact date for the Minoo paperwork she would have to turn in on their way home but that was why she was there.

While she was at all of that, head together with Kimiko, the neuter attendant ran back up the dock and spoke to a young child who'd not yet chosen their gender. That child ran off into the city so his escort could come and collect him. Probably not what Aunt Colleen would want but she really did have a great many responsibilities with the ship and this was Aravel's task, not hers.

Only someone in the line direct from Tamura Tao could do this.

He rather hoped that Kimiko never found out that he'd lied to her. There was so much more that he needed to accomplish than a simple informal visit. Great-Uncle Jarmon had been very firm about what Aravel had to do while they were in Masumi City. He even had a list of questions, long since memorized, that he needed to answer.

First and foremost, could the Dana relocate out of Aingeal to Chinwendu without losing their fortune and their ships to the regulations of the Chinwenduese government?

Because with the way things were going in Aingeal, there was every likelihood that they would be driven out in the next ten years.

2. CONFLICTING MANDATES

Watching Ravi walk away, blithely chatting with the little neuter the Tamura had sent to escort him, had made Colleen's teeth ache. Her jaw, too. Damn them, didn't they understand how important Aravel was? To send just a child, barely twelve, to walk him through the streets was an insult. It was almost a threat, not that Aravel seemed aware of it.

No, that boy was perfectly happy to take every scrap of freedom he could beg, bargain for or steal and then run with it. Laoise was going to break her neck if something happened to Ravi. She'd damned near done it before they left port back home.

"Breathe," Captain Bryna murmured. "The Harbor Mistress is coming our way. You don't want to give her cause to search us."

Colleen breathed, slow and deliberate, as she continued to mark off barrels as they were unloaded from the *Harmonious Song*. She watched the Harbor Mistress form the corner of her eye and yes, that was a woman who'd take anything she could get. You would have thought she was Delbhana from the rolling, confident strut up the dock. That smirk was a dead ringer for… a Delbhana smirk.

Huh.

After this little encounter was over, Colleen was going to have to ask a few questions. Maybe grease a couple of palms. The Delbhana were working quite hard to steal the Dana markets from them. It would make sense for them to come after Chinwendu. Their cheap silk from other parts of the world wasn't ever going to compare to the real thing from Chinwendu and the Dana imported the best of the best. Everyone in Aingeal knew it.

Undercutting their position in Chinwendu by allying with one of the families here would do a lot for making that possible.

If, of course, the Delbhana allies managed to combine Delbhana bluff and plotting with Chinwendu politeness and politics. Colleen didn't think it was possible but who knew? Maybe the Delbhana had a genius hidden away somewhere who could do it.

And the Ladies might rise up out of the Strait to carry them all back to the Morrigan's arms where they'd all live in perfect peace and happiness.

Colleen snorted and then shook her head at Captain Bryna's curious look. "Sometimes my mind runs in circles."

"Everyone's does," Captain Byrna replied before switching to a low murmur. "She's definitely coming our way. Ito Aina, one of the Tamura's least favorite people. Watched her pretend not to interrogate Ravi before he left. She's a sly one."

"Reminds me of Lady Etain, actually," Colleen murmured back. "Too much confidence, not enough intelligence and flexibility to back it up."

Before Ito Aina had even introduced herself, she snapped her fingers at Colleen. Then pointed at the clipboard Colleen was using. Colleen stared back, making no move to pass the clipboard over.

"Papers," Aina demanded.

"You are?" Colleen asked in a similarly hostile though not quite so belligerent tone.

Aina's lips went thin as she glared. "Harbor Mistress. I require your paperwork, sailor."

"I am not a sailor," Colleen said, ignoring the out-thrust hand Aina pushed at her. "I am Dana Colleen, second daughter of the fourth daughter of the Dana Clan. I speak with for the leader of our clan Dana Laoise. You are?"

Speaking for Laoise gave Colleen higher rank that a mere Harbor Mistress and the truth of that made Aina's cheeks go blazingly red. She kept on glaring, kept her hand out as if just demanding the clipboard was going to work. So Colleen stared right back, trusting that eventually the sheer awkwardness of Aina breaking all the Chinwendu social protocols was going to take its toll on her.

"All foreign sailors are required to submit to inspection of their paperwork," Aina finally snarled. "Papers. Now."

Colleen shrugged, tucked the clipboard under her armpit, and then pulled out the Minoo paperwork that identified her as a member of the Dana Clan. Tucked into that little packet of seals and careful initials marked with double-checked dates was the single sheet that identified her as far as the Chinwendu government was concerned. If only the Minoo would be satisfied by something that simple.

"Here," Colleen said, passing the Chinwendu ID over. "My paperwork."

"The rest?" Aina said without looking at Colleen. When nothing happened her eyes snapped up to Colleen's face. "You risk arrest."

"No, I don't," Colleen replied with a little laugh despite the fact that every single sailor in the area, every official, ever dock worker had stopped to watch their confrontation. "Minoo law requires that I do not ever pass that identification over to another person. You are breaking the law. In several ways. As well as being shockingly rude. I still do not know your name and rank, *Harbor Mistress.*"

The derisive tone that Colleen put on 'Harbor Mistress' made Aina's breath hiss between her teeth. Not that Colleen was wrong. She wasn't. Aina was completely in the wrong in this encounter and everyone knew it.

Strangely, it felt so much like being back at home on the dock by the Dana Clanhouse that Colleen almost expected to turn around and see Laoise strolling up the dock to see what the fuss was.

Probably closely followed by a Delbhana woman intent on making the trouble that much worse.

"I am Ito Aina, Harbor Mistress for Masumi City," Aina snarled at her. "I require all your papers and that clipboard be turned over to me. Now."

"On what authority?" Colleen asked.

She made sure that her voice projected. In a port, surrounded by water, that was an easy thing to accomplish. With the deeper tone Colleen had used, her voice boomed, drawing looks from everyone, even people up on the shore.

This area of the port went so quiet that Colleen could hear the crabs clicking their claws underneath the dock as they ate algae off the pylons. Aina's chin came up but her lips were too tight, too white, for her to be as confident as she was pretending to be. Her fingertips trembled, too. Colleen breathed slowly and caught the scent of fear-sweat coming off Aina.

Oh yes, this felt just like home.

Damn it.

"I am--"

"A Harbor Mistress does not have the unilateral authority

to seize a sailor's papers unless they are guilty of the commission of a crime." Colleen cut Aina off before she could start spouting nonsense about her authority as the Harbor Mistress. She made sure to use the same booming tone of voice. "Guilty of a crime, not suspected of one. You are not the law, Ito Aina. You are not one of the Guard, charged with apprehending suspected criminals. You are not a Judge, assigned with the responsibility of determining guilt or innocence. And you most certainly are not a ruler, responsible for determining the fate of the guilty. You are a Harbor Mistress and you do not have the authority to take my papers or anyone else's!"

Colleen shouted the last bit while snatching her Chinwendu ID back from Aina.

Who gaped and backed off a step while going pale. Her hands came up to make the bow of extreme apology but then snapped back down to her sides as if someone had just poked her in the side with a very sharp knife.

"This is not over," Aina hissed, low and quiet so that her voice wouldn't carry.

"Excuse me," Colleen replied, loud and proud and glaring for all she was worth, "could you repeat that? I didn't hear you. Harbor Mistress."

The flinch was worth every bit of the snarl Aina gave her. Aina stomped up the dock, pushing past the dock workers who'd stood frozen through the entire confrontation. Strangely, she didn't accost anyone else. Not a single sailor or dock worker, not even the obvious foreigner from Ntombi with her ink-black skin and thick dreadlocks spiking off her head.

"Targeted," Colleen murmured to Captain Byrna.

"Oh yes," Captain Byrna agreed as she waved everyone back to work. "Very much so. I find myself very curious what sort of gossip we'll get this evening in the taverns and bars."

"Me, too."

Not even eight months ago, Colleen's last visit to Masumi City had been a marvel of politeness and manners. She hadn't spoken to the Harbor Mistress but Colleen was fairly certain that Ito Aina wasn't the one who'd had that job before.

Something had changed. Something very major had changed. And she needed to find out what it was.

Unfortunately, Colleen also needed to keep Ravi safe if she wanted to keep from getting thrashing at Laoise's hands when they got home. Damn it. She should have fought Ravi about splitting up. If anything, she should be the one going up to Tamura Manor to talk to everyone there, not Ravi. He was just fifteen.

But then he couldn't do the paperwork that was her personal responsibility and Ravi apparently had a mission of his own.

Next time she shipped out she was going to insist on a sit-down meeting with everyone involved so that they could get all their stories straight before they left port. Since she hadn't gotten that, she'd have to sit Ravi's butt down and have him tell her what he was up to, too. Bring Captain Byrna in on it, get everything out in the open.

Yes, that's what she'd do.

Once she had all their cargo off-loaded. And then all the paperwork for Chinwendu filled out. Oh, and then submitted to Ito Aina who would poke every single hole she could in it just for sheer irritation's sake at this point.

So maybe tomorrow. Probably tomorrow, given Colleen's luck.

Damn it all.

She shook her head and focused back on what she had to do. Just like always. Take care of the little details and the big picture took care of itself. No matter what, Colleen would have to account for every single barrel and bale of silk to the Minoo authorities. Not to mention to Great-Uncle Jarmon.

So she'd get this done, all of it accurate as Colleen could make it. And then she'd fight her way through Ito Aina's obvious agenda. Fortunately, Colleen could read Chinwenduese as easily as Aingealese so there was no way for Aina to trip her up on misquoted law and regulation.

Yeah, she'd cope with this. But then she was nailing Ravi's twinkling toes down so that she could find out exactly what was going on. Only once she knew could she take steps to keep the situation from getting worse. And right now it looked like Ravi was the one who had all the real information.

He'd share it or so help her she was going to spank his bottom.

FIGHTING the Morrigan's Hand is now available at all major retailers in ebook and TPB format.

OTHER BOOKS BY MEYARI MCFARLAND:

Day Hunt on the Final Oblivion

Day of Joy

Immortal Sky

A New Path

Following the Trail

Crafting Home

Finding a Way

Go Between

Like Arrows of Fate

Out of Disaster

The Shores of Twilight Bay

Coming Together

Following the Beacon

The Solace of Her Clan

You can find these and many other books at www.MDR-Publishing.com. We are a small independent publisher focusing on LGBT content. Please sign up for our mailing list to get regular updates on the latest preorders and new releases and a free ebook!

AFTERWORD

Covid-19 messed with the world.

It also messed with me. This story was supposed to come out in March 2021. Then it slid to June. Then July. I finally got it published in September 2021.

When you go through trauma, as the world did in 2020 & 2021 or as Duru did in his story, it has so many effects on you. The way you think, the way you react, what you see as possible or stare blankly at for the longest time before giving up and turning away…

For most of 2020, I soldiered on with my writing. The publishing limped along but I kept going. 2021 was supposed to be better.

It wasn't.

Around March 2021, things went pear-shaped in my head. I could write words. I could not publish them without a month-long struggle.

Around June 2022, seemed to be clearing up for me but it was deceptive. I couldn't't quite get anything done no matter how hard I tried. By November I had grand plans.

Then my mom got deathly ill.

She died 2 months later at the end of January. I spent the rest of 2023 accomplishing very little on the creative side of things.

Now, as 2023 ends and 2024 begins, I'm getting back at it. I give no guarantees as I'm going to be kind to myself. But I'm excited finally.

That said, I'm so very relieved to get this story out to you at long last.

If you want more stories like this one, please go sign up for my newsletter on www.MDR-Publishing.com. You'll get updates on whatever I've got coming up, special deals and you can get a free ebook or collection of my short stories. Or you can sign up at my Patreon and get access to my art, writing and whatever's going on creatively in my life.

Thank you for reading!

Meyari McFarland
    January, 2024
    www.MDR-Publishing.com

AUTHOR BIO

Meyari McFarland has been telling stories since she was a small child. Her stories range from adventures appropriate to children to erotica but they always feature strong characters who do what they think is right no matter what gets in their way.

Meyari has been married for twenty years and has no children or pets. She lives in the Puget Sound, WA and enjoys the fog, rain and cool weather that are typical here. When vacation times come, she and her husband usually go somewhere warm like Hawaii or they go on their own adventures to Japan and other far away countries.

Her life has included jobs ranging from cleaning motel rooms, food service, receptionist, building and editing digital maps, auditing and document control.

MORE FROM MEYARI MCFARLAND

Website:

. . .

MEYARI MCFARLAND

www.MDR-Publishing.com

SOCIAL MEDIA:

Patreon - https://www.patreon.com/meyarimcfarland
  Mastodon – https://wandering.shop/@MeyariMcFarland
  Pillowfort - https://www.pillowfort.social/Meyari
  Facebook   -   https://www.facebook.com/meyari.mcfarland.5
  Pinterest - https://www.pinterest.com/meyarim/

If you enjoyed this story, please leave a comment on your favorite site. Also, please sign up for the newsletter so that you can hear about the latest preorders and new releases.

www.ingramcontent.com/pod-product-compliance
Lightning Source LLC
LaVergne TN
LVHW042003060526
838200LV00041B/1859